CHAPTER ONE

SL

I squint my eyes and le
small black writing on
some stupid reason, my vision is a ...

Parker, one of my best friends and business partner, tries to get my attention from across my desk. "Slade?" He puts another handful of sunflower seeds in his mouth. The sound of him slurping and chewing is enough to drive any man to drinking. Even at this early hour.

"Hmm?" I ask, keeping my eyes on the screen. I squint more, but it doesn't help me with the fine print. "How do you turn the brightness down?" I mumble more to myself than him. *I hate this computer!* Angel got it for my thirty-second birthday a few months back. Said it was state of the art. The creme de la creme. What-the-fuck-ever. It sucks.

I look away from the screen and over to Parker as he spits some sunflower seed shells into a white Styrofoam cup. "Can you go do that somewhere else?" My voice is clipped; I'm in no mood for him today.

A few pieces fall onto his black fitted shirt that looks like he bought in the kid's department at the mall. He feels the smaller he buys them, the bigger he looks to the women. I think it makes him look like an idiot. Doesn't matter what the guy wears, women still flock to him. This is the reason he is the only one not settled down out of all of our friends.

"What's wrong with you?" he asks as he dusts off his shirt, pushing his leftovers onto the floor for the cleaning lady to pick up later.

I ignore his question as I sit behind my desk. What's wrong with me? I have a few answers to that question. It could be the fact that I think I'm going blind. Maybe I do need contacts like Angel has been saying. Could be because I got no sleep last night. It could be 'cause of a little foot that kicked me in the balls three times. Could be because a little hand slapped me in the face twice.

See, Angel is letting Sadey sleep with us. At first, I didn't mind. But that was back when she was a tiny little baby who didn't move much. She had a little white wedge that kept her in one spot and protected her, so we didn't roll over onto her. Now she's fifteen months old and is just like her mommy—constantly rolling around in bed. No bed would be big enough for all three of us. Oh and you can't forget Peaches. That damn dog loves to lay across my legs. The other morning I got up for work and almost fell flat on my face due to the numbness. That dog needs its very own room.

"Don't you have something you need to be doing?" I question him while I still look over my screen.

"Nope." His chipper voice is quite annoying as well.

UNCHANGEABLE

an undescribable novella

bestselling author *Shantel Tessier*

adjective: **unchangeable**

not liable to variation or able to be altered.

UNCHANGEABLE

I look up to see my office door open as Tate, my other best friend and brother-in-law, walks in. He plops down in one of the black high-rise chairs next to Parker. "Please tell me I can beat the shit out of someone today?" He fists one hand into the palm of another.

"The day is young." We have a party that we are working tonight. Some big rig who works in the oil industry is having a party for his closest three hundred friends. They hired us to be security.

The security company we have isn't exactly 'traditional.' I know when others think of a security team, they think a bald headed man with a beer belly standing in the center of a mall. That's what I think, anyway. But that's not what we do. We do mainly private parties. Very upscale private parties. Parker's father is the mayor of St. Louis and has kept us busy. I guess some would think that we're not qualified for this type of job considering none of us went to school for this, but I would disagree.

Parker has plenty of skills that he brings to the table since he is a cop. Tate is just Tate. He can just look at you and it would scare you shitless. He's the first to throw a punch and the last to go down. He towers over most, and the tattoos that run up and down his arms would make you think twice about fucking with him.

And myself, I have lots of connections from being a defense attorney. People talk about how ruthless I was in the courtroom and how many cases I won. Now that I've jumped the fence and want to help those who aren't always guilty, they want me.

It's a win-win.

"Man, you two need to get laid," Parker chimes in leaning back in his seat talking to Tate.

"Speaking of laid..." Tate quips, looking over to him. "That bitch you had over last night...?

He gives a chuckle before he responds. "That bitch would be Sarah. She was fun."

"I'd say. I could hear her in my room. Can't you go sleep with them at their house?" Tate growls. Tate invited Parker to move in with him about two years ago. Back then, they were both single. But now that Tate is engaged, I think things have changed.

"Wow. You both are very pissy this morning. What's the problem?"

"You will be the one with a problem if you don't quit bringing all these girls home. I have to hear about it twenty-four seven from Missy."

"Why does she have a problem with it?" Parker asks all defensively.

"You're joking, right?"

Parker shakes his head. "What?"

Tate sighs. "Nothing. Just be careful with who you bring home. That's all."

Parker nods his head in some sort of understanding. "Noted."

The door to my office swings open once again and in walks our assistant. Angel and I both took off when she had Sadey. And I had left Tate and Parker to hold down the fort for a week. That was a mistake. I came back to having an assistant. I was going to fire her, but Angel talked me out of it. She thought it was a good idea and thought I should at least give her a chance. Turns out, she was right. Who knew?

"Hey guys," she says as she walks up to my desk. I smile up at her. Tate mumbles his hello, and Parker all but whistles as she walks past him. I catch him staring at her ass through the clear view of her black pants. I clear my throat in warning. If something were to happen between them, I would have to fire one of them. Guess which one I would keep?

"Glad someone is happy today," Parker says as he leans back in his chair with a smile on his face. His eyes run up and down the back of her, taking in her small curves and curly blond hair. If I had to be honest, I would say I have grown quite fond of Krystal. Do I think she is pretty? Sure. Do I find myself attracted to her? No. I have come to look at her almost like a sister. Parker, however, wants to fuck her. After her first week here, I had to give her a dress code. She wasn't dressing bad or anything, but I just felt like I needed to lay some ground rules. After all, a girl covered in a trash bag could turn on Parker.

Krystal frowns. "Is there something wrong?" She looks down to me. "Is Samantha and Sadey okay?" Over the last year, she has become real close with Samantha. They do regular girl shit together. Like spa days and the gym. She even watched Sadey for a few hours while I took Angel out on our anniversary.

5

"No, they're fine. I'm just tired." I wave her off. Now that Parker has set down the sunflower seeds, I'm better. "What do you have for me?" I ask looking down to the papers that she holds in her hands.

"Yes, Krystal," Parker smirks. "What do you have for me?" He wiggles his eyebrows and it makes me nauseous.

Tate reaches over and slaps him on the arm. He just chuckles as Krystal giggles. The poor girl. If she only knew how serious he was. He would eat her alive and spit her out. Good thing she is engaged. And if you didn't know her as we do, all you'd have to do is look at the huge-ass rock on her left hand. Her dad is in financing, and she's marrying his best friend's son. They all have money. She actually quit working for her father to work for us. Said she needed some different scenery — whatever she meant by that. I'm thankful.

"This is your schedule for the week. I have printed off copies for all of you. Tate and Parker, yours are on your desk waiting for you."

"You're too good to me," Parker jokes, and Tate rolls his eyes.

"Thank you," I say taking them from her and placing them on my desk.

She nods her head and turns around, shutting the door behind her as she leaves.

"Are you trying to get us sued?" Tate asks Parker.

"I'm just playing with her." He laughs. "I

wouldn't really fuck that. She's engaged, and I'm sure, out of the two of us, Slade would fire me."

"I would," I say with a smile of my own.

"Slade?" I look up as the door opens again. Krystal pokes her head in. "Sam is on line two."

I nod my thanks and pick up my office phone. "Hey, beautiful." Parker makes a choking sound that I ignore.

"Did you get my emails?" she asks sounding like she's out of breath. My dick starts to get hard at that thought. Our sex life isn't as exciting as it once was. It used to be romantic, and we would take our time with foreplay. Now, when we do it, we usually have to hide in the closet from our daughter. Or the other day, we did it in the back seat of her SUV while it was parked in the garage. And it's usually a quickie. Real exciting, I know. But as both parents and running a company, there's just not much time for us to hang out as a family, let alone have sex as much I want it.

"Why do you sound so out of breath?" I ask.

She gives a half laugh. "I'm out of breath because I just helped Courtney bring in two hundred pounds of sugar. Those bags are heavy. But enough about sugar. Did you get my emails?"

"Yes." I sigh. "But I haven't had a chance to look at them."

"Slade." She takes a deep breath. "I need to know which fabric you want. I have to place the order by five tonight."

"Order for what?" I hate to admit it, but I sometimes forget what she tells me.

I can feel her aggravation with me grow over the phone. "The curtains. I sent you emails of different fabrics that I think will look nice with the new furniture."

Ah, the new furniture that she just had to have last week. If I didn't know her better, I would think she is going through a nesting stage. She went through a big one right after she had Sadey. But I think that only happens when a woman is expecting. I'm not a hundred percent sure. "I will look at them and give you an answer by lunch," I say already pulling up her email.

"Thanks. I gotta go. Love you."

Click.

I hang up the phone and start to read the email. "Holy shit!" I say in surprise.

"What?" Parker demands.

"She sent me over fifty different links to choose from." I was thinking like maybe three. My wife is very picky and when she finds something she wants, she gets it. I'm surprised she can't narrow it down.

"Just pick one," Parker says with a wave of his hand, and I arch an eyebrow in question. He sighs. "Do you think she really wants to know what you like best? She's gonna choose what she likes best. So, just pick one."

I hate to admit that he has a point. I slide the mouse over the selections and pick one.

My cell phone starts to ring. I reply to her email with the number that I chose and pick up my phone. "Hello?"

"Slade," comes my dad's voice. "I need a favor, son."

CHAPTER TWO

Samantha

"Courtney?" I yell over my shoulder as I stand in the back of the bakery making my third batch of scones for the day.

"What?" I hear her yell from the office.

"Did you ever find out what happened to our shipment of packaging supplies?" I ask, hoping she has an answer for me.

Our shipment never arrived yesterday and after several phone calls and a few yelling matches, I found out that our delivery truck had an accident. Apparently, there was a twelve car pileup on the freeway, and our truck was involved. I felt like a terrible person for causing such commotion over freaking supplies. Thankfully, they said that he was gonna be okay.

She makes her way out of the office and comes to stand beside me. "I spoke with them about an hour ago. They said that there is a new truck on its way with our supplies. It should be here by tomorrow afternoon." She then blows a few loose strands of her blond hair out of her face. I know she's exhausted. Twin boys will do that to you, yet it hasn't affected her job. When I hired my best friend, she pretty much just worked up front, taking orders and greeting customers, but now she runs the back.

She does all my inventory and keeps the books. Missy still runs the front, and Holly helps me with all the cooking. The bakery that I started because of my mother is a success, but it wouldn't be that way if I didn't have all of them helping me out.

I sigh. "Do we have enough until then?"

She nods. "It'll be close, but I checked after I got off the phone with them and we should be okay. If not, I will think of something."

I laugh at her idea of just being able to make something work. "Just keep an eye on it and let me know when you think I should start to panic."

"Will do, boss," she says before she reaches over and grabs a muffin from the counter. She turns around and walks back into the office.

I get back to my scones when the door that separates the bakery from the back swings open. I smile as I see my half-brother, Tate, walk in followed by Parker. "Good morning," I say cheerfully.

"Morning," Tate growls.

"It is a beautiful morning, isn't it?" Parker says with a smirk on his face. I guess he got laid last night. He's usually not a morning person.

"Everything okay, Tate?" I ask turning to face them as they sit down at the round table that they always come in to occupy. I swear our guys can eat as much baked goods as our customers.

"Fine," he mumbles as his eyes slide over to Parker quickly. It makes me think that they are fighting over something. The fact that Missy now lives with them has to be hard on their friendship. I love all my girlfriends to death, but I couldn't imagine any of them living with us. But I would for sure be the first to welcome them into our home if any of them needed it. I can just understand how hard it would be a couple to live with a bachelor.

Parker leans back on the back legs of his chair and places his hands behind his head. His cocky personality is in full force today, and it's not even ten o'clock yet. "Don't let him fool you. He's a little pissy."

"Is there something I can do?" I ask.

"Nope." He reaches over and shoves Parker in the chest. Parker's hands and feet go flying as his chair tips back and he goes crashing down to the floor. Tate finally cracks a smile. "But Parker just did."

I try to hide my laugh as Parker picks himself up off the floor followed by his chair. "Fucker," he mutters before sitting back down — with all four legs on the floor.

"Where's Slade?" I ask, looking back to the door wondering why he hasn't come in yet. He must still be up at the office.

"He was on a phone call," Parker responds as he dusts off his shirt. "We were being too loud." He does air quotes around too loud. "Told us to get the fuck out of his office so we just left."

Slade and the guys bought an office a couple of doors down from Angel's bakery. So, they show up here quite often. "A new job?" I ask. I couldn't be more proud of Slade. Changing his life for me and Sadey. Changing his life for himself. It's been hard work, but he is proud of what he does. Thankfully his mother, Vivian, doesn't work and watches Sadey for us. I didn't want to have to put her in daycare. I was thankful and heartbroken all at once when she offered to watch her. My first week back at work, I cried like a baby. Vivian assured me that Sadey was just fine. She sends me pictures of her throughout the day. Sometimes I FaceTime her. Other times Vivian brings her up to the bakery when they are out on one of their shopping trips.

"Hopefully," Parker speaks. "The bastard needs to beat the shit out of someone. Maybe that will help his shitty mood."

I frown. "Slade's in a bad mood?" I didn't get to talk to him this morning. I rarely do in the mornings. I have to get up early to open up the bakery by five am. Slade sleeps in, gets Sadey up and ready, and drops her off at his parents' house on his way into work. But I didn't get that he was in a bad mood when I called him about my emails. I mean busy, yeah, but not hateful.

Tate kicks Parker under the table, and Parker squeals like a child. "Is this beat up on Parker day? Jesus," Parker growls as he leans over and rubs his shin.

"If you continue to talk, yes!" Tate spits out.

Parker goes to speak but closes his mouth as the door opens once again. Finally, I see my brother crack a real smile when his fiancée walks into the room. "Hey, sexy," she says sweetly with a naughty smile on her face.

He pats his knee and she goes over to sit down on it. He slides his hand through her long blond hair and lowers her ear to his face as he whispers something into her ear. She giggles like a little schoolgirl, and Parker rolls his eyes as he lets out a heavy breath. I think public displays of affection drive him crazy. Whenever any of his buddies are showing any kind of affection to their wives, he acts like it's putting him out. If you ask me, he's jealous.

"What's up, Missy?" I ask placing a smile on my face.

Her smile grows and her blue eyes shine when she looks over at me. "Are the scones ready? We are just about out."

"Yes," I say spinning around and picking the tray up off the counter.

She gives him a kiss on the cheek and then stands from his lap. "Here you go." I hand them off to her.

She thanks me and then turns, walking out of the room, telling Tate over her shoulder that she loves him. He goes to say it back, but the door has already shut.

"Yuck. You two make me nauseous," Parker says with a look of disgust.

Tate's face has lost that smile, and he looks angry all of a sudden. "You make me nauseous, fucker," he growls. Tate shoves his chair back all of a sudden and stands as he grabs his phone out of his pocket. "Motherfucker," he mumbles before he turns and shoves the back door open before he walks into the back alley.

"Well… this has been an eventful day, and it's not even lunchtime," Parker says before he goes to stand as well.

"Are things not going well with you and Tate?" I ask. Parker and I have never been real close. I hated the guy when I first met him. I was afraid that he was gonna show Slade what he was missing by being with me. Parker's free. He sleeps with all the chicks he wants. Slade was once that way. But over the last year and a half, Parker and I have become closer. I think him saving mine and Sadey's life brought us closer together. He's still an arrogant idiot, but he has shown me several times that he will do anything to protect his friends. I'm glad to know that he considers me one of them. Although I would never tell him that. It would just make his head bigger and no one could deal with that.

"Not that I know of." He shrugs. "He's just in a bad mood. Doesn't mean I did something to put him there."

"I know," I respond. "I was just wondering. I just got this vibe that he was mad at you over something."

He shakes his head as Tate walks back into the bakery. "Come on. We gotta go," he calls to Parker as he storms through the front door.

I go back to my cooking and pull out everything that I need to make some muffins when Missy comes into the back. "Do you know what that call was about?" she asks as she approaches me.

"No. He didn't say. He took the call outside. Why? What's up?"

"I don't know," she says softly as she looks down at the floor. "Our wedding is in two weeks. And I think it's stressing him out."

"Weddings can do that to you." I agree with her.

"I think…" She stops herself for a second. "I think he's worried about his mom coming in. You know."

Tate and his mother don't have the best of relationship, but I thought they had worked that out. "Didn't you guys go and spend some time with her up in Alaska?" I ask.

She nods. "We did, but at times it just felt off." She lets out a heavy sigh. "Tate has come a long way but you know how much it takes for him to open up to someone. I know he loves her, but I think he wants to fight it."

I pull her in for a hug, and I rub her back softly. "It's gonna be okay." She buries her head into my shirt, and I hear her sniff. I pull away to look down at her, and she quickly wipes her eyes.

"He's taking it out on Parker." So that is why he was being a dick to Parker today. "Parker keeps bringing women home and I feel like Tate wants that. Like he looks at my name he had tattooed on his ring finger and wonders why he ever fell in love with me in the first place." They both have worked so hard to get where they are today. Missy was in love with Tate for years. I can see where she would be afraid to lose him. And Tate just recently allowed himself to love her. Although I know he's loved her for just as long.

"Missy." I place both of my hands on her face and force her to look at me. Her blue eyes look so sad. "Tate does not think that way about you. He loves you. I saw the way his face lit up when you walked into the room. But if you honestly feel that way, you need to talk to him. You need to tell him what you're feeling." I've been there with Slade way too many times. Where I kept my feelings to myself, afraid he would be mad at me. In the long run, we both got mad and ended up fighting.

She sniffs one more time and slowly nods her head. "Right now," I say, and her eyes widen. "You take a break and call your soon-to-be husband." Before she can object, I spin her around and give her a little push to the back door.

CHAPTER THREE

I reach over my desk and turn my lamp off. I look over at my clock on my desk, and it reads a little past midnight. The party that we worked went really well and thankfully didn't last too late. Yawning, I grab my jacket that's hanging over the back of my chair and close up my office. I walk down the brightly lit hallway and make a right. I open the door to Parker's office to tell him bye but pause when I walk in to find him lying face down on his desk. His mouth half open and snoring. Red Bull cans and wrappers from protein bars litter his office. He seems to be the messiest. And I don't know why, we have a cleaning lady that comes in and cleans. There's no way he can destroy his office space this much on a daily basis.

"Parker," I call out. "Go home and sleep." I keep hearing him mention getting a couch for his office. This must be why he wants one.

His head shifts a little bit and he reaches up to rub the drool off his mouth but doesn't respond to my demand.

I chuckle and shut the door behind me. "You can just sleep here," I mumble. The guy runs on little sleep as it is. He helps run our company during the day and works four nights a week as a cop. He's like his damn cat, Puss Puss—taking little cat naps throughout the day. One day it's gonna catch up to him.

I walk across the hall and open Tate's office door. "I'm out," I say leaning into his office.

He looks up from his computer and holds up a finger as he talks into his phone. "Okay. See you in a minute. I love you." He hangs up his phone and nods his head to me. "I'm on my way out as well." He pushes a few keys on his keyboard and then pushes his chair back. "I'm gonna go join Missy for a drink up at Larry's." "Missy wants to go to the bar?" I ask. She's not much into drinking or the bar scene.

"Guess she has some friend that is having boyfriend trouble and she wants me to come up there for a little bit. Wanna join us?" he asks.

A beer does sound great. It's been a long-ass day. I look down at my watch. I know Angel and Sadey are already asleep. Not like I'm going to see them anyway. "Sure," I say.

"Where's Parker?" Tate asks looking around the hallway. "He said something earlier about wanting to go out as well."

I point over to his office. "He's passed out, drooling and snoring on his desk."

Tate rolls his eyes and then starts to walk down the hall. "His loss."

"Is everything okay between the two of you?" I ask as we walk to our cars.

"Yes." His clipped answer leads me to believe he's lying.

"Is everything okay with you?" I push a little more.

He stops walking and looks over at me. "Yeah." I catch him as he looks down at his ring finger where he had Missy's name tattooed. "Everything is *now*." I don't know what he means by now, but I don't push him anymore.

We get to Larry's, and thankfully, it's dead this time of night on a weeknight. I don't come here much anymore. Even after Angel and I started dating, we still went out a lot together. Not so much now that we have Sadey. If for some crazy reason, we both have a night off we spend it together at home. And I would choose that over anything else in this world.

I follow Tate to the table that sits in the back corner. I smile when I see a little blonde stand from the table. Tate pulls Missy into his arms and gives her a kiss before they sit down.

"I was surprised when Tate told me that he was meeting you here," I say as I sit down.

"I'm just here for moral support," she says with a smile. And I guess she is referring to her friend even though we are the only ones here at the moment.

"Well, how have you been?" I ask. I know what Missy and Tate went through was hard at times. But I knew he loved her. I knew they would end up together. I smile to myself. Boy, do I love being right. As Angel would say, it doesn't happen often.

"Good," she says with a smile. Tate places his

tatted arm over her shoulder, and she leans closer to him. "Just staying busy."

"Started school yet?" Missy had dropped out of school after we returned from Vegas about two years ago. But I know she wants to go back and finish.

She shrugs. "I'm in no rush. I really enjoy the bakery. And Sam takes good care of me." She looks up at Tate. "Is Parker coming, too?"

He shakes his head. "He fell asleep up at the office."

She laughs. "And you guys just left him there?" She asks.

"Yep." We say in unison.

She sits up and pulls her phone out of her back pocket as it chimes. She reads a message and then smiles. "Katherine should be here any minute."

Tate frowns. "Is that the girl we went to her house and fed her huge-ass dog?"

"Yeah. She and her boyfriend are on the rocks. She said she needs a few drinks."

"Missy…" he warns as his eyes harden down at her.

"I couldn't blow her off."

I watch them bicker back and forth in confusion. What have I missed?

Just then, a waitress comes up to our table. I order a Bud Light and Tate does the same. Missy orders a water. "A water??" I ask. "Why aren't you drinking?" Missy isn't a big drinker. She definitely hates beer. But it's not like her to not have a glass of wine that usually takes the entire night for her to drink.

Her cheeks turn red and she looks over to Tate with a nervous smile on her face. "Well…" She drags out the word making me wonder what is going on.

"Well, what?" I ask when she doesn't say anything else.

"We're pregnant." Tate's words freeze me where I sit. I watch as he reaches out to her and gently touches her cheek before giving her a soft kiss on the lips.

"Pregnant?" I repeat in a high pitch tone. "I didn't know you guys were trying." Did I? I guess Angel could have mentioned it once and I just forgot, but I can't imagine forgetting something that important.

"No. That's what's so great about it. It just happened," she responds, and her big blue eyes light up.

I feel a huge smile spread across my face. I stand from the table and pull Tate from his chair. I give him a big brotherly hug and slap him on the back. "Congratulations," I say. Tate had come a long way from what he was when I first met him. He was always angry. Always looking for that next fight. He still has his moments — I think we all do — but falling in love with Missy is the best thing that could have happened to him. She reminds him every day that he is worthy of being loved. And I know in return he loves her with all that he has.

I pull away from him and walk over to Missy. It's so weird to hug her small frame. "That's amazing. Congratulations," I say, and she sniffs.

"Thank you. Please don't tell everyone just yet."

I know they are probably worried. Hell, when I found out Angel was pregnant my world went into overdrive. Trying to prepare yourself for a child is like trying to prepare yourself for a thunderstorm. And this is her second pregnancy. I can only imagine what she is going through after she lost their first.

You think nine months is forever away, but it will be here before you know it and then you're like fuck what all did I forget?

"I won't," I assure them as I find my way back to my seat. "But how long have you known?"

"We just found out a couple of days ago," she says excitedly. "I haven't even been to the doctors yet. But as soon as I do, I will share the news with everyone."

I watch as she cuddles up next to her soon-to-be husband once again. And I can't help but feel their excitement. Here is a couple who couldn't be more different than night and day. Tate is rugged and dark. He's not the kind of guy you look at and think he looks scary but is probably a teddy bear. He is far from that. He has always worn his hatred and darkness for all to see. But when Missy is in the room, he lights up. He smiles at her. He talks sweetly to her. It's truly amazing what love can do to someone. If you ask me, it saved him, and he knows it.

"There you are."

I hear a woman's voice and look up over to the table where a tall brunette stands.

"Katherine," Missy says and stands to give her a hug. "I'm so glad you called me."

Katherine pulls out a seat and plops down into it. "Yeah, well, I could use a beer," she says looking over to me. "Katherine," she introduces herself reaching out her right hand to me.

"Slade," I say leaning over to shake it.

She tilts her head for a second as if she's thinking about something. Then she places her elbow on the table and points at me. "Is your wife Samantha?"

"Yes," I say slowly wondering how this woman I have never met knows my wife. The only woman she hangs out with I know very well.

She smiles. "I've met her. I go into her bakery every now and then."

"Oh, yeah?" I say leaning back in my chair. "I've never seen you up there before."

"I work the night shift up at the hospital. I go by there on my way home sometimes."

"Katherine and I met while in nursing school," Missy informs me.

"Where's the boyfriend at? Is he going to show up here and make a scene?" Tate asks her with narrowed eyes.

"I don't know and I don't care," she says with a shrug of her shoulders.

"Did you guys break up again?" Missy asks with a frown.

"Not that I know of. But that doesn't mean we won't be before the night is over with," she says with a laugh.

I sit in the back of the bakery with Tate on my right and Parker to my left. Tate is hung over. Once our drinks came last night, we all toasted to the secret yet exciting news. Missy and her friend, Katherine, were the first to leave. Tate and I stayed a little longer to have a few more beers than we should have.

Parker chugs back a Monster; he looks like he just woke up. "Did you sleep all night at the office?" Tate asks him.

"No," he says as he stretches. "I woke up about four thirty this morning and went home." He rubs the back of his neck. "I have the worse crick in my neck. Why didn't you guys wake me up?"

"I tried. You were snoring and drooling. It wasn't pretty." I reach out and knock him on the back. "You should have come out. It was fun. Plus, you missed Missy's hot friend who came out with us." I wouldn't consider her hot, but I like giving

Parker shit!

He moans as if he's in agony. "I missed a chance to get laid?" he whines.

I laugh. "No one said she was that easy."

"They're all that easy," he says before placing his head on the table. Tate and I both laugh at him.

We all turn our heads to look over at Angel as she drops a box onto the floor making a loud noise.

"Need help, babe?" I ask, already standing from the table.

"Nope," comes her clipped voice.

Parker sits up and turns to look at me with a smirk now on his face. "You're in trouble," he whispers, and I sit back down in my seat ignoring him. She's not mad at me. I haven't done anything. I didn't stay out too late last night. Not like I closed the bar down. And I sure as hell didn't do anything with Missy's friend.

I left the bar a little after one. She was fast asleep when I got home and was up and gone by the time I woke up. Just like I thought she would be.

"What are you guys doing up here?" Holly, who married my brother a couple of years ago, asks as she walks in from the front. She just announced a while back that she is expecting their first child. I swear pregnancies are running in the water here.

"Just hanging out," Parker says before he shoves a cookie into his mouth.

"Hmm," she responds. "I'm gonna start

charging you if you continue to eat everything Sam makes."

Parker speaks through a mouth full of cookie. "So worth it."

We all laugh.

Angel stabs a pair of scissors through the tape on top of the box and slices it in half, before tossing them up onto the counter. I sit back and watch her carefully as she yanks supplies out of the box and places them on the counter. Holly takes the few things that she needs for the front and exits the room. Missy comes into the back and is on her cell phone talking quietly as she heads off to the back office. She gives Tate a little wink that makes him smile back at her.

Parker continues to shove food into his mouth as if he hasn't eaten in days. I reach over and slap him in the back of the head.

"Ow," he whines through his cookies. "What was that for?"

"For being yourself, Parker," I say as I stand from my chair. I walk over to Angel and place my hands on her shoulders to stop her from destroying another box.

"What, Slade?" she snaps causing me to frown.

"Is there something wrong?" I ask running my hands up and down her arms. She sighs heavily. "Tell me what's wrong."

She looks over at Parker and then back to me but doesn't say anything. I grab her by the hand and pull her through the back door of the bakery and into the alleyway. She shivers as she crosses her arms over her chest to protect herself from the cold.

I wrap my arms around her and pull her into me. "Am I the reason that you are in a bad mood?"

"Yes," comes the one word that I was expecting.

"What did I do?" I ask truly wondering this.

"What time did you get home last night?" She wastes no time with the questions.

"I…"

"You went to a bar. Instead of coming home, you went to a bar."

"With your brother and Missy. It was just…" I try to explain to her that it was just for a drink but I did have more than one.

She pulls away from me. "I don't care who it was with. You chose a bar over coming home to your family." She sniffs and her bright green eyes start to tear up.

"Whoa," I say wondering where this is coming from. "Why does that bother you so much?"

"Really?" Her voice rises in anger. "Why would I get mad that you chose a bar over your family?"

"It wasn't like that," I say softly. "It was just a few drinks."

She closes her eyes as she takes a few deep breaths. "I just don't wanna be that couple."

"What couple?"

"The one where the husband would rather go to a bar to pick up chicks than come home to his family." Her words make me realize what has her so upset and I'm shocked that she could even think like that.

I walk up to her and place my hands on her cold cheeks. I lean down, placing my forehead on hers. "I'm sorry, Angel. I didn't think it would upset you."

She wraps her arms around my neck. "Parker told me you were in a bad mood yesterday. I wanted us to spend some time alone together last night," she whispers. "But you never came home and I fell asleep waiting for you."

I hate that I let her down. I guess in a way I can see where she thinks I chose to go out rather than come home but that was not my intention. "Let me make it up to you," I offer.

"How?" she asks softly.

I smile against her lips. "Tonight. I'll do anything you want me to do tonight. I'll close up early and the girls can close up the bakery. We can go home and be alone. Just you and me."

She sighs. "That sounds wonderful but what about Sadey?"

"I'll have my parents keep her a little later than usual. Then after we have our time together, I'll go and pick her up. Deal?"

"Deal."

I lean in to kiss her, but she pulls away when she hears my phone ring. "One second," I say pulling it out of my pocket. *Father* lights up my screen.

CHAPTER FOUR

I leave Slade to his phone call and walk back into the bakery, mainly because I'm freezing cold. February in St. Louis can be brutal.

I find Parker still sitting at the round table looking off into the distance. "Tired?" I ask. I overheard them talking about him falling asleep up at the office last night. I can relate to him quite a bit. I feel like I'm tired most of the time. I have moments where I just want to fall to the floor, curl up into a ball, and sleep for days. Slade and I got lucky with Sadey. She has always been a baby who enjoys her sleep. But work is just kicking my butt. You would think that I would be used to my schedule by now, but I'm not.

"Yeah," he says through a yawn. "Working the night shift at the department is killing me."

"Why don't you quit the force?" I ask leaning against the counter. I don't know all that much about Parker when it comes to his career as a police officer. I know he's good at his job, and he has saved his friends' lives. I just don't know why he's still there. I guess he could need the money.

He looks up at me at my question. His dark eyes look intense for someone who is so tired. He looks to be thinking about the right thing to say but is having a hard time finding the right words. "For as long as I can remember, I've always wanted to be a police officer. It would be silly to throw that away now just because I'm tired." And with those words, he stands from the table and walks out.

I have a feeling there's more there than what he wants me to know. Parker is always cutting up and being an ass, but I feel like he's covering something up. He doesn't want others to know just how vulnerable he truly is.

"Hey baby, I gotta go," Slade says as he comes through the back door.

"The office?" I ask, and he just gives me a nod. "I love you," I mumble against his lips as he leans down to kiss me. His lips barely touch mine and he goes to pull away. I wrap my arms around his neck and pull him into me. He gets the hint and opens up his mouth for a deep kiss. This man, the same man who asked me to have a three-way with him in the women's bathroom, still has the power to bring me to my knees with a kiss.

His hands slide up my back; he opens his mouth wider and deepens the kiss. Allowing me to taste. I moan as my insides tighten and my legs start to turn to mush. I need him so bad. My body needs him. I need to be reminded what loving him feels like. All too soon, he pulls away. "Sorry, Angel, but I gotta go," he whispers, breathing heavily.

I slouch back against the counter and watch him leave. The muscles of his back move as he slides his coat over his shoulders. My hands tingle at the thought of touching him. At ripping that white shirt off his body and placing my hands on him. I need him on top of me so badly I can taste it. In a matter of seconds, he's gone and I sigh.

I catch sight of Missy walking out of the office now off the phone and I stop her. "Did you talk to Tate?" I ask.

"I did." She smiles. "And thanks. Everything is better now."

I nod my head at her, not bothering to ask any more questions.

Once I head into the house, I throw my purse along with a jacket on the back of the couch as I walk through the living room. I then kick off my shoes as I make my way down the dark hallway. It's a little past ten now. Slade had called me earlier and apologized, saying he couldn't take off early today. He mentioned something about his dad and then said he would call me back. He never did. He did text me that he would pick up Sadey from his parents' and see me at home later, but that isn't unusual.

I come into our bedroom. I come to a stop when I see an open suitcase sitting on the end of our bed. My heart pounds in my chest and a million thoughts are going through my mind at the moment. "Slade?" I all but yell.

He comes out of our closet. "Shh," he hushes me

as he walks over to the bed and drops a pair of dress slacks into the suitcase. "Sadey is asleep."

"What in the hell are you doing?" I ask wide-eyed staring at the suitcase.

He takes a deep breath and then walks over to me. "I have to leave."

"Leave? Where do you have to go?" I don't remember him ever mentioning traveling with his new company.

"I've been helping my dad on a case." I look up at him and my confusion grows as he speaks.

"Case? When did you start helping your dad with a case?" Has he been working cases this entire time? "I don't understand," I say trying to figure out what I have been missing. Our lives have changed a lot in the last two years. Our family has grown, and we have started new careers. There are days I wouldn't see him unless he comes by the bakery for a snack or my cookies. We used to stay up all night having sex; now sex is the last thing on my mind when I lay down at night. My head barely hits the pillow, and I'm out like a light. But that doesn't mean he can just up and leave without letting me know what the hell is going on.

He gets my attention as he looks down at me, his big blue eyes are soft, and he runs the back of his hand down my cheek. It's like he's trying to soften the disappointment that he knows is about to come. "My dad called me yesterday and wanted me to help him on a case. I wasn't going to tell him no."

I pull away from him in shock. "When were you

going to tell me that you were helping him out?" I demand, placing my arms over my chest.

He runs a hand through his dark hair. "It wasn't that big of a deal."

That's his excuse for everything lately. He used it for going out to the bar instead of coming home as well, and frankly, I'm tired of hearing it. I stomp over to the bed and point to his open suitcase. "This isn't a big deal?" I ask and my voice trembles from anger.

"I have to leave, Angel," he snaps at me.

"Why can't your dad go?"

He throws his hands out to his side as if that was a horrible suggestion. "Because he put me in charge of this case."

"Oh," I exclaim. "You're in charge," I repeat with a bite. "Why the hell are you in charge of a case in the first place, Slade? This isn't what you do. You're no longer an attorney."

"This is exactly what I do," he shouts furiously, and I take a step back from him. I sit down at the end of the bed with a heavy sigh, and he takes in a calming breath. I hate how quickly a conversation can turn to a fight these days. But that's what happens when you are stressed and lacking sleep.

After a few tense seconds, he walks over to me. Kneeling down, he speaks. "I'll only be gone for one day."

I can't help but hate this. I thought he gave this up for us. For him. I never asked Slade to quit his job as a defense attorney. He loved it. It was part of him, but when he walked away from it, it was like a weight was lifted off us. I felt safer. He felt more secure. But it's only been a year and here he goes running back. I hang my head and twiddle my thumbs as they lay in my lap.

He places his hand on them to calm my nerves. "What if this one case makes you want to go back?" I say the only thing that I can think of. Slade and I haven't always been the best at saying what we feel. I kept stuff in afraid of how he would react, and he kept things from me because he felt I couldn't handle the truth. It was exhausting and frustrating how many secrets we once had. I don't want that between us. How will we ever grow as husband and wife if we continue to stay secretive?

He lifts his hand to push my hair back out of my face. "You and Sadey mean more to me than anything in this world," he says with a frown as if I should already know this. And I do. "More than a case. More than my company. You two are my life, Angel." I swallow hard waiting for the but. There's always a but. "I'm just helping out my father. It's only a day. I'll be back before you know it."

I nod my head, accepting the decision he has already made. "I'm gonna miss you." I sniff. It's gonna be weird to be in our house without him here. Even if it's only for one night. Slade and I have never spent one night without each other since we've been married. It's crazy how much you can depend on someone.

He gives me a reassuring smile. "I'm gonna miss my girls. I'll be back before you know it." He stands and gives me a soft kiss on the forehead. "I'm gonna take a quick shower," he says before walking into the bathroom.

I lie down, place my head on my pillow, and close my eyes as I yawn, praying that everything he says was the truth.

CHAPTER FIVE

Samantha

I sit in the back of the bakery at the round table that the guys usually occupy thinking about our fight we had last night and my morning. Slade left first thing this morning to head to Chicago. He hugged and kissed me and Sadey bye. I cried and he reassured me there was nothing to be sad about. I almost felt like he was ready to leave. To have a break from our busy lives. Like it may feel like a mini vacation for him. I just had this feeling that something wasn't right, and I was right. I just got off the phone with him. He has to stay another day. It broke my heart. I said *okay* because there was nothing else to say. He's working a case, and I have no control over what happens to it. He didn't sound excited about having to stay an extra day, but he also didn't sound hurt either.

I just can't get it out of my mind but I feel like our spark has run its course and that scares me. I love Slade more than anything. He's my world. But how do you keep that feeling alive? How do you not let everyday life and children come between the two of you? How do you keep the romance alive? That is the million-dollar question.

I lay my head down on the table and sniff. The tears threaten to fall, but I close my eyes tightly. I'm just begin emotional. Lack of sleep and a mind that won't stop from coming up with the worse scenarios will do that to you.

"Wakie, wakie."

I let out a sob when I hear Parker's voice. I don't know why, but I just want to be left alone. Today is that type of day that you cover yourself with blankets and stay in bed. But that's not a possibility when you have a child and a business to run.

"Hey?" I hear him walk over to my side before his hand lands on my back. "What's wrong?"

Another sob wracks my body when he speaks. "Samantha?" His voice gets more demanding than concerned. I fight him as he tries to pull me to sit up but eventually I lose.

"What is going on?" he asks kneeling down in front of me.

I shake my head quickly as I wipe the tears from my face. "Nothing."

"You're lying."

More tears fall. Is Slade lying? I mean, I know it's a business trip but is he going to go to a bar there by himself? Will he meet someone who makes him feel the way I used to? Someone young and pretty with no cares in the world? I was once that girl. Hell, that was me about two years ago. Most couples date for years, get married and then wait a few more to have kids. Our relationship moved so fast.

"Is it because Slade left town?" he asks, and I can't help but nod my head.

"He didn't even ask me to go," I say sadly. "Sadey and I could have gone up there with him. He just called and said he has to stay another day. It is Valentine's Day, after all." Tomorrow is Valentine's Day. He said he would be back by tomorrow afternoon. But I would have loved for me and Sadey to have gone up there tonight and stayed with him. Guess he didn't feel the same.

"Shit," Parker hisses softly as if he just realized tomorrow is Valentine's Day. I'm pretty sure Slade doesn't know that. I just remembered it this morning after Slade walked out of the house. Which is crazy because I have been preparing for it for the last month up here at the bakery.

"Let me help you," Parker says running his hands down the side of my arms.

"You can't."

He stands and looks down at me. "I can. Let me watch Sadey. You can leave tomorrow morning and come back on Sunday. It will be one night." He smiles softly down at me. "If I have any problems, I have plenty of friends to call."

"I can't...Tate and Missy..."

"I live with them. They can help me if I need it." He bends down, grabs my hands, and pulls me to stand. "You can and you need to." He sighs as if he's thinking how to say the next words. "I don't know what's going on, but it's serious, Sam." I sniff. If someone like Parker who is too consumed with himself can see his friend is having marriage problems, then it is obviously bad. "But go and surprise your husband on Valentine's Day."

I'm at a loss. I need to see my husband. I need to talk to my husband and I need to do it without Sadey around. The girls can run the bakery just fine without me for one day. I don't want her to hear us fight, and I don't want to do something stupid that will wake her up. Somehow the universe has sent me Parker to save my marriage and my sanity. Oh God, I'm gonna barf.

Slade called me five times today. And text me about twenty. He was overly sweet and sounded in a much better mood, but I couldn't help think that it was because of the case. He's getting to do what he has always loved. I wasn't making him smile. Or making him laugh, and that is what hurts me the most.

My plane ticket has been bought. My bag is packed. All I need is a good night's sleep, but I can't close my eyes. I keep thinking about Slade as I lay here in our bed. Our little princess lays sleeping beside me. I wonder what he's doing. If he's working or sleeping. If he's getting a drink out at some bar or if he's thinking about me.

What is going to Chicago going to fix? When we step off that plane on Sunday, we go back to our busy lives. Life isn't a vacation. And marriage isn't easy. I could work up at the bakery twenty-four hours a day but being a parent will still be my hardest job. Even when you're not with your kids, you worry about them. And I guess that never changes even once they are married themselves.

I lean over and give her a soft kiss on her little cheek before I lie back down. I don't know what the future holds for Slade and me, but I know that I'm gonna fight to keep it.

CHAPTER SIX

I lift the cold glass of bourbon to my lips and take a sip. I inhale sharply at the burn before placing it back on the bar.

"Another one?" the guy asks standing behind the bar.

I shake my head no as I pull my phone out of my pocket. I look at my phone. It's almost one here so I know Angel is in bed back at home. I set my phone down and pick up my drink once again. I need to finish it off and then go up to my room. It's been a long day, but thankfully, it was a productive one. I ended up having to push my stay back to another day. In light of new evidence, we get to go before a judge tomorrow. Angel didn't sound all that surprised when I called her this morning, but she did tell me she understood. What did she want me to do? I can't leave. My father asked me to help him out on this job because my brother is swamped with cases and my parents had planned a trip this weekend months ago. For what, I can't remember. I just know they were going out of town and this case has moved quicker than he could have anticipated. So, of course, I was going to help them.

"Is this seat taken?"

I look over my shoulder to a woman who stands

there pointing to the empty seat next to me. Her brown eyes are covered in a dark shadow. Her lips tinted red. I can't help but stare at her plump breasts that she has popping out from her red dress.

"No. Go ahead." I stand and pull my wallet out of my back pocket about to pay when she speaks again.

"Don't leave on my account." She smiles up at me flirtatiously. I know that smile. I used to get it all the time. And before Angel entered my life, I would have flirted back. Said something witty and then tried to rip her dress off. Times were simpler back then. You only had to please one woman for an hour at a time. Fuck them and then leave. Now I have to please the same woman every second of every day. I'm starting to understand that that may be a losing battle.

"Early morning," I respond pulling a twenty out of my wallet. I place it on the bar and slide it over to the bartender. He goes to walk away with him, and I inform him to keep the change.

"You look like you could have used another one." As she speaks to me, her brown eyes look me up and down. After they run up the length of my jeans, they take in my fitting black shirt. She licks her lips as if she wants to do just that to me personally.

I clear my throat to get her to look me in the eyes. "Have a nice night," I say dryly before I turn around and walk out of the hotel bar.

I want to see that look in my wife's eyes. I want her to need me as much as I need her. But that's just me being childish. Letting shit get to me. I miss them both so much. Since the day she had Sadey, I have always kissed her goodnight. Didn't matter how tired I was or if she was already asleep, I always read her a book. She's my world. The world that Angel allowed me to have, and no matter how imperfect our marriage is, I would never screw that up.

I lie in my cold and empty hotel bed as I look at pictures on my phone. I have pictures from my and Angel's wedding. Her beautiful smile, bright green eyes, and her dark hair. That white dress. My heart stopped the minute I saw her enter that church as she started to walk down the aisle to give me everything she had.

Now I'd give everything I had to go back and relive that day.

Today has been productive. Crazy yet productive. The meeting with the judge took up my entire day. I step out of the cold taxi and make my way to the very fancy, expensive hotel. I find myself slowing down as I pass the hotel bar, but I would prefer a shower more at the moment. I can come back down afterward.

I called Angel once again as I exit the elevator to my room. I spoke to her earlier this morning and she seemed off. More than normal. But, of course, she told me it was nothing. I didn't believe her but didn't press the issue. I could hear Sadey crying in the background, and I didn't want to stress her out more than she already was.

I walk into my room and throw my phone on the king-size bed when her voicemail picks up. I'll call the bakery after my shower.

The shower helps cool my hot skin down. I just wish I could turn my brain off.

I just wrap my towel around my waist when I hear a soft knock on my door. "Coming," I say walking out of the bathroom. I had just called room service before I got in the shower for some new towels. They really should stock more of them in each room.

"That was fast…."

The words stop flowing when I see my wife standing at the door to my hotel room, in Chicago. Her long dark hair is down and in big curls. She's wearing a pair of black jeans and a white sweater. Her bright green eyes light up the second she sees me. "Angel?" I ask surprised.

"Surprise," she says softly as she gives me a nervous smile.

I look down at her hands. Her left hand holds a bag and the right hand is empty. I lean out into the hall and look around. "Where's Sadey?" I ask looking around once again. I'm confused to why my wife is standing at my hotel room with a bag.

"I'm here alone," she says stepping into my hotel room.

I shut the door behind and turn to face her. "By yourself? Who has Sadey?" I ask trying to think of who could have her. My parents? No, they're out of town. That's why I'm here in the first place.

"Don't get mad," she whispers. "But Parker has her."

I throw my head back and laugh out loud. "Good one," I say smiling. She looks down to the floor and starts to bite on her bottom lip nervously. "You were joking right?" I ask. *She can't be serious.*

She shakes her head slowly. "You gotta be kidding me," I say still laughing.

"No." The words are softly spoken.

I stand there and stare down at her. "You left our daughter with my best friend who calls his cat Puss Puss?" She nods. I turn around giving her my back. Shit, this is bad. Very bad. "What the fuck were you thinking?" I demand half shocked.

"She's fine."

I can't believe she's saying this. "How do you know?"

"Because I trust him."

I laugh darkly. "You don't trust him for shit!"

"It's just one night. And he has Missy and Tate to help him."

I run my hands through my hair confused. "Why would you leave our child behind?" I ask trying to understand her. "Why the hell are you even here?" I demand as my anger grows as I realize why she has ignored my calls all day. She knew I would have told her not to come.

She fists her hands down by her side, her anger growing as well. "I'm trying to save our marriage." Her voice rises with anger but by the time she's done her eyes start to fill with tears.

"Save our marriage?" I whisper as my confusion grows. "What are you talking about, baby?" I take a step toward her, but she takes one back.

"Come on." Her voice cracks as she begs me to understand "I feel it." Her green eyes start to get watery, and it tears at my heart. How could I ever let her think our marriage needs saving? "I know you feel it, too." I place my hands on either side of her face. "Tell me you feel it," she whispers.

I place my forehead to hers and I swallow hard before I answer her question. "Yes."

She sniffs and I pull her away from me so I can look down at her. "I can feel your fear, Angel. And I'm so sorry to have put you through this. Our marriage may not be perfect, but it doesn't need saving."

She pulls her face out of my hands and wipes the tears from her red cheeks. "When you chose a bar over going home to your family then there's a problem, Slade."

"It was only a couple of hours." I don't see the problem.

"You chose that one drink over us," she says through gritted teeth.

"Why are you so mad about that? I don't understand."

"I'm mad because I stayed up waiting for you to get home," she seethes finding her anger. "I'm pissed because I wanted some alone time with you." She starts crying again. "And by the time you came home, I pretended to be asleep just so I wouldn't have to touch you. What kind of marriage is that, Slade?"

"You pretended…? You told me you fell asleep."

"I lied," she says with shame, and she covers her tear streaked face. "I love you," she mumbles into her hands before she drops them. "But I was once that girl in the bar, Slade. I was the girl who made you smile. Who made you happy. Now I feel like you try to avoid me on purpose." She lifts her hands and gestures to my hotel room. "When would you have ever left me at home while you went out of town?"

"I've had to go out of town for jobs before."

She shakes her head as tears run down her cheeks. "That's the thing. This isn't your job."

I step up to her and wrap her in my arms, holding onto her tight now afraid she may turn around and walk right back out that door. Her body shakes as she cries into my chest. "I love you. Angel," I whisper leaning down to kiss her head.

"You didn't tell me about helping your dad." She sniffs. "You didn't ask if me and Sadey would come here with you."

"I didn't think you two would want to travel on

a business trip with me," I say truthfully. "Especially with Sadey."

She pulls away from me, and I'm reluctant to let her go. "Do you even know what today is?" she asks, and I shake my head slowly. "It's Valentine's Day," she cries, and I feel my heart drop out of my chest. "It's Valentine's Day and I left our daughter back home with your crazy friend because I felt being here with you was more important." She cries again. "What kind of mother does that make me?"

I run a hand through my damp hair. "I'm so sorry I forgot." My voice is barely over a whisper. I knew Valentine's Day was coming up but somehow I pushed it to the back of my mind. Her words interrupt me and I suddenly find myself placing my hands in her hair, making her look up at me. "You are an amazing mother," I say truthfully. "And you're a wonderful wife," I add. "But there's no need to worry. I'm not going anywhere. I love my job I have now. I'm only here because my dad asked me."

"Why couldn't he get someone else to do it?" she asks.

"I've worked with this guy before." Repeat offenders were once very common for me. This guy just happens to be addicted to alcohol and pills. His daddy, however, has the money to get him out of anything, but he needs an attorney to represent him.

"I'm sorry." She swallows. "I just panicked. I thought..."

"Don't think." I lean down and press my lips to hers for a soft kiss. It's the first time I've really kissed my wife in days. And I can see where she thought that I was pulling away from her.

Angel has taught me a lot. And on thing is that a kiss can say more than words. When I kiss her, it's like the world is right. Like no other people exist.

CHAPTER SEVEN

Samantha

I can't get enough of him. My hands wrap around his neck, and I push my body into his. I moan into his mouth as his hands find their way into my hair. My nails scrape down his naked back, and he shudders.

I pull away from him, breathing heavy. I don't waste any time as I pull my shirt up and over my head. His lips are back on mine within seconds. He starts to walk me backward to the bed as I feel his fingers unclasping my bra. "Please?" I beg between kisses.

He pushes me onto the bed and then crawls on top of me. "Please what?" he asks, raising his eyebrows in question.

I smile to myself. "Please," I say desperately. "Fuck me." I arch my back and cup my breasts. He grabs my wrists and pins them down by my head. I push my chest up loving the feel of his skin against my sensitive breasts.

He lowers his face down to mine. "And fuck you, I will." He lets go of my arms and slides down my body. He rips off my jeans and pulls his towel off allowing me to see how hard he is for me. My heart races and my breath comes quicker knowing what he is going to give me. He then yanks my panties down my legs, and I help kick them off.

Before I can even take a deep breath, he's back on top of me. His hand finds its way between my legs, and I arch my back as he thrusts a finger roughly inside of me.

He growls as his face nuzzles my neck. "Need you so fucking bad," he says. He removes his finger and replaces it with what I really want.

I arch my back as he pushes himself all the way into me. Letting me feel the stretch that I love so much. "Need…you too," I pant as he pulls back and thrusts forward once again.

He drops his head to the crook of my neck and softly bites my already sensitive skin. I cry out as my nails dig into his back. He growls at the sensation and I dig them into his ass, trying to pull him in deeper.

He lets out a moan and then reaches back to grab my hands. He wraps his big hands around my wrists and holds them down by my head, and I suck in a deep breath. I arch my back and he bends down gently kissing my nipple before biting down on it.

"Oh. God," I hiss as he continues to thrust into me. This is what I've missed. This is what I wanted from Slade in the beginning—just sex. But somewhere in the last fifteen months, we have lost it. I don't want to be one of those couples who don't make time for one another. Just because we've added to our family doesn't mean we have to forget about one another.

"Fuck, Angel." He groans before his lips attack mine. I can feel the desperation, the desire that he has for me, and it makes me need him even more.

"How is she doing?" I ask Parker over the phone, as I lie naked in Slade's hotel bed. I couldn't go another second without knowing what my little princess is up to.

"She's fine," he says through a mouthful of food.

"What are you doing?" I ask turning over onto my back and looking up at the ceiling while Slade brings our room service cart over to the bed.

"I took the little princess out for ice cream."

I go to speak but hear a woman's voice on the other end of the line. "Well, hello there. She is adorable."

Parker chuckles "Thank you."

"Is she yours?"

"Yes." He sounds like a proud father but I know he's just trying to use my child as chick bate.

I sit up quickly. "Parker..."

I hear Sadey giggle in the background, and I roll my eyes. I can't have my child subjected to this.

"Okay. I'm back," he says after a few seconds. "Damn, she's better than Tate's motorcycle," he says excitedly, and I don't even bother to ask what he's talking about. I feel like I already know too much.

"Oh and I seem to have a problem."

"Just one?" I mumble to myself.

"I have to go into work tonight, so I just wanted to let you know that I will buckle her car seat in the front seat next to me."

"No." My heart pounds in my chest at his statement. *I need to get back now.* "You can't take her..."

"You're right." He pauses for a second. "Maybe I should put her in the back. Much safer back there."

Where the criminals sit? "Parker..." My voice trembles with fear.

His laughter cuts me off. "I'm just fucking with you," I growl. "You really don't trust me much, huh?"

"Here." I hand the phone over to Slade. "You talk to him," I say placing my hand over my chest. I'm pretty sure he just gave me a heart attack.

I lay there with an arm over my face as Slade chuckles and talks to Parker about work stuff. I really feel like I made a bad decision. I shouldn't have come here. I shoot up off the bed and start looking for my clothes. I can get back tonight. Sadey won't have to spend the night with Parker.

"I gotta go. I'll call you later," I hear Slade say as I find my underwear on the floor. I go to put them on, but Slade grabs me and spins me around. "What are you doing?" he asks, snatching the panties of my hand.

"I'm going home. I'm sure I can catch a flight tonight."

He shakes his head. "Relax, Angel. Sadey is fine."

My mouth drops open. "He said…"

"I know what he said. He told me. He was just messing with you." He smiles. "I trust Parker, babe."

"With your daughter?" I ask in shock. "You didn't earlier," I remind him.

He smiles as he runs his thumb over my bottom lip. "You trusted him this morning and now you don't?"

"That's because I wasn't thinking. Clearly, you're not thinking."

He leans down, placing his lips to mine. "Know what I'm thinking?" His minty breath runs over my face, and I break out in goosebumps.

"What?" I ask breathlessly.

"I'm thinking…" He reaches down and grabs my thighs. He lifts me up and I squeal as I wrap my legs around his waist. "I'm ready for round two," he says before his lips are on mine.

EPILOGUE

Life isn't perfect. It's not supposed to be. How would we ever appreciate the good unless we experienced the bad? Angel and Sadey are my good. They will always be the things that I got right, no matter how many things I do wrong.

I can't help the big smile on my face as I sit on Tate and Parker's couch while Parker sits on the floor with Sadey and my wife. They laugh as Tate tells us how Missy had to show him how to change a diaper while we were away.

"I had it figured out," Parker says defensively.

"You had it on backwards," Missy argues with him from the couch beside me.

"Hey. It was my first time to ever change one." He leans down giving her little nose a kiss. "I was gonna Google it to make sure."

Angel laughs as she places our daughter in her lap as she continues to sit on the floor. "Well, you need to learn anyway for when you have kids."

Parker's face turns white as a ghost. "Now, you know me better than that."

"Parker can deny it all he wants, but you know he'll be the one who ends up having five kids," Tate adds laughing at his own statement.

"Abso-fucking-lutely not," he says shaking his head quickly. He reaches over and picks up his fat cat off the floor. "Puss Puss is the closest thing I'll ever have to a child."

"Kitty," Sadey says reaching out for Parker's cat.

Parker's eyes light up. He drops his cat and reaches over and picks Sadey from Angel's arms. "Oh, my God. I taught her that. I kept saying it over and over last night."

We all laugh. I don't tell him that she's been saying kitty for a while now. I'll let him have this moment—because this is one of those moments that makes you feel like you could rule the world. Love and children have a way of doing that to you. And I can't wait for my best friend to experience what I have. A love like that remains unchangeable.

A SNEAK PEEK FOR READERS INTO

PARKER'S BOOK!

UNPREDICTABLE

bestselling author *Shantel Tessier*

BLURB-

I'm known for being an asshole. It suits me. I'm that guy who jokes about love and how settling down is overrated. Why would a guy ever fall for one woman when he can have as many as you want? Makes no sense to me.

But if being a cop has taught me anything, it's that life is unpredictable. And that is exactly what Katherine is. The woman makes me question my sanity on a daily basis. Sometimes she makes me want to keep her to myself; other times, she makes me want to jump off a cliff just to get away from her.

Yet I still find myself turning into that little pussy I said I'd never be. Showing up on her front door holding flowers, only to have her throw them at me. Calling just to say hello, only for her to press ignore. Yeah, I've become a pussy all right. A whipped one at that. At first she was a challenge, but now I don't like the fact that she is playing hard to get. But when someone comes after me, threatens my job, my life. It's her that stands by my side. It's her who has to pay for my sins. And it's her who I'm threatened to lose. One thing that you need to know about me is that I'll fight for what I believe in. And I believe in her more than myself.

What's that saying? Boy meets girl and the rest is history...Well, those who fuck with what is mine, will become history

CHAPTER ONE

I turn off my headlights and lay my head back against the headrest as the brown haired woman bobs her head up and down on my hard cock. Her technique could use some work but who am I to judge? I've never sucked a cock before, and I sure as hell don't know how many 'suckers' she has licked. All I know is that I have one and she is willing.

"Sandy," I breathe as I run my hand down her back and over her ass. *God, I wish she could take her jeans off.* My cop car isn't the most convenient place to get some action, but I got called in tonight and I already had plans to meet up with her. So here we are, on the side of the road, making the best of it. And hey, I'm actually pretty comfortable. She's the one stretched out over my center console with her knees propped up in the passenger seat. I realize I could get into deep shit for doing this while I'm on duty, but no one is gonna catch us way out in the middle of nowhere.

"Hmmm?" She hums around my dick, and I sink my nails into the soft denim of her jeans that cover her ass. I just wanna spank the fuck out of it as she begs me for more.

"2388 we have a 10-50 at I-55 and LaSalle Park." The second the voice comes over the radio informing me of traffic incident, I sit straight up, shoving my cock all the way to the back of her throat and knocking her head into the steering wheel.

"Parker," she chokes out as she jumps up off me and grabs her head. I place my hand on her chest and shove her back into the passenger seat as I reach for the radio.

"2388. 10-84 is 15 minutes."

I hang up the radio and start buttoning my pants. "What? You're leaving?" she pouts.

"Yes. I'm on duty," I growl at her sounding annoyed.

"What about us?" she questions in a child-like voice and pushes her bottom lip out.

I lean over and grab her hair. I yank her to me and plant my lips on hers. I kiss her deeply, and she moans into my mouth as she rubs her hand over my still hard cock that I shoved into my pants. I pull away and she pants. "Meet me at my house in an hour." She knows where I live. This isn't the first time we've hooked up.

"Give me your key," she demands. And I shake my head. "Why not?"

I have roommates. I originally moved in with Tate. Then Tate fell in love and his fiancée who now lives with us. She would have my head if I allowed a girl to have my key. I can already picture Tate calling me while Missy is in the background yelling at Sandy to get the fuck out. Then I'd be kicked out. And that is just not gonna happen.

"Just meet me there in an hour," I repeat, and she nods her head reluctantly.

I give her one more kiss and then all but shove her out of my car. She's parked right behind my cop car so I'm not worried about her having to find a ride. I make sure she gets into her car before I take off down the darkened road that I had her meet me at. It's pretty late at night, or early morning, however, you wanna put it.

Within seconds, I'm turning my sirens and lights on as I'm jumping on the highway. Papers scatter across my dash and my sunglasses slide from one end to the other as I take the curves sharply. Another five pass by quickly as I fly down the road. I look at my clock that reads almost six thirty in the morning. The sun still hasn't come up, but it won't be much longer. This will be my last call. Once I'm finished with this, I will be off duty. But the funny thing about a call is that you have no idea how long it will take.

CHAPTER TWO

Katherine

I stand in my hooker heels and little slutty, denim shorts with my arms crossed over my chest, trying to cover up my hard nipples. It's freezing in this room. I shouldn't have dressed this way in the first place — not only do I look like I belong on Eleventh Street, but I also don't even match. But clothes are the last thing on your mind when you have to rush the only man you've ever loved to the hospital.

Releasing a heavy sigh, I lean forward and place my forehead on the cold glass. A chill runs down my back. I close my eyes and try to think happy thoughts. None comes to mind. Don't get me wrong, my life isn't a disaster by any means. I just can't think of anything to give me hope at the moment. Hospitals will do that to you. They have a way of sucking the life out of you. Which is weird for me to say, considering I work at one. It's different though when you're at one because of a family member.

I open my eyes and look out the now fogged window due to my breathing. The lights of St. Louis still glow as the sun starts to come up in the distance. I look down to the streets and watch all the people drive to work, preparing themselves for another busy day at the office. Their boring, repetitious lives.

I never found myself to be normal. My father

always told me that I was special. And as a daddy's girl, I believed him. I still do. Don't take that as me being conceited. I'm not! My definition of special has just changed from when I was younger.

"Miss?"

I turn around to see a nurse in dark red scrubs that I don't know standing at the door to my father's hospital room.

I nod my head as I look over to my father. Lying there sleeping from the medicine he was given after his fall. It scared me to death. All I heard was a loud crash and then found him lying at the bottom of my stairs. I don't even know what he was doing on the second floor anyways. He laid there lifeless in a puddle of blood and glass that broke from the pictures he pulled off the wall as he looked for something to grab onto for support.

My eyes go back to hers and I catch her as she looks me up and down with a look of disgust on her face. Judging. For my lack of clothing. She probably thinks I'm his mistress or some over exaggerated bullshit. People really do have overactive imaginations these days.

I clear my throat and straighten my shoulders. "Is there a reason why you're in here?" *Bitch*, is probably her next thought, and she would be totally right. What can I say? I may be a daddy's girl, but I'm very much my mother's daughter. *Total bitch!*

"I was just going to give you these." She reaches out her hand, and I now realize that she holds something in it.

I take them from her, and my eyes scan over the material. "A home?" I ask once they register.

She nods. "I wanted for you to look over your options."

I throw them over onto the chair that holds the only thing I was able to grab as I stormed out of our house. My cell. Which is dead — piece of shit. "There is only one option," I snap at her.

She actually looks surprised by my words. As if I was just going to throw him into a home and forget about him until he died and collected his money. Dress like a hooker, people will think you're a gold digging whore just waiting for an elderly man to give you his life earnings. What is the world coming to?

"I understand you want to…"

"No, you don't," I interrupt whatever bullshit she was about to come up with. "I have taken care of him for the last year. I'm not going to stop now."

"He needs twenty-four hour care," she reminds me.

"You can't tell me anything that I don't already know."

She's quiet for a few seconds. "Can you be there twenty-four seven?"

A simple question should be given a simple answer. But the answer is no. I work. That's all I do, but it takes up most of my time.

She gives me a warm smile at my silence, and I want to fucking punch her lights out. I've had to take anger management before. I really don't have time for it again.

I look back over at my father and walk over to him. I can feel her eyes staring at my exposed thighs, and I sit down on the chair next to his bed to obscure her view.

"You don't have to make a decision right now. He will be here for a while." With that, she walks out and leave us alone.

I grab his cold hand and take it in mine. "No worries, Daddy," I whisper to him. "You're not going anywhere." And I mean that. I'll do whatever I have to do. I'll hire someone. Hell, I'll move someone in to take care of him while I'm gone.

My throat tightens and I feel the sting of my eyes but I push that feeling back.

Be strong, Katherine. Keep your eyes open. You never know when the lights will go out.

That's the only thing I ever remember my mother saying to me. She spoke those exact words the day she walked out on my father and me. I was six. My father raised me, she was never really there anyway. And that's what makes this even harder. I should be taking care of him now; I shouldn't be giving up on him.

I run my hand softly over his silver hair. My dad has changed a lot over the last two years. He went from being a man to being a toddler. I've had to bathe him, feed him, and dress him. The list never ends. I went into nursing because of him and now I feel like I'm just pawning him off on another.

I lean down and give him a kiss on his cold cheek. "I'll be back tomorrow, Daddy," I say, and I feel a knot start to form in my throat, but I swallow it down. *I don't cry.*

Pulling up to my house, I grab the pamphlets and my dead cell phone. Once inside, I go into my kitchen and throw them onto the kitchen table.

"So…"

I jump and spin around throwing my back up against the fridge with my hand over my racing heart. "What the hell are you doing here?" I snap.

Leaning up against the countertop in my kitchen stands my ex-boyfriend.

"Why the hell are you here?" I ask narrowing my eyes on him. He looks like fucking shit. His longer blond hair is slicked back into a low ponytail. His white shirt looks dingy and his ripped jeans are hanging so low that if I were standing behind him I would probably be able to see his ass crack along with his boxers. What can I say? I know how to pick them.

He reaches up and runs his fingers through his blond beard. "To get my truck."

I shake my head. "I already told you. You're not taking it." I might have bought that truck for him, but it isn't leaving here. "Coming here won't change my mind."

"Well, if you'd answer your fucking phone then you would know that I've been here for three hours, and I'm not leaving until you give it to me." His voice rises as he speaks.

"I was busy."

His chest rises and falls as he tries to calm his anger. He looks around and then his eyes are back on mine. "Where the hell have you been anyway?" he demands as his eyes look over all my exposed skin. They actually darken when they rest on my chest. He still hates the fact that I got them done. But he learned a simple lesson—never tell me I can't do something. His eyes finish their descent down my stomach and then legs. He reaches down to adjust himself and I roll my eyes.

"None of your business," I respond turning away from him.

"Where's your father?"

"He's gone." I throw over my shoulder.

"He died?" His voice softened at his question, and I hate it. He doesn't give a flying flip about my father or how I feel.

"My father is also none of our business," I say refusing to answer his question.

Just as I go to step out of the kitchen, he speaks. "You put him in a home!"

I spin around and see he has found the brochures on the kitchen table. He's holding one in his hand as he skims over it.

"Of course, you did," he says before I can respond. "I've been telling you to do that for two years and the moment you break up with me, you get rid of him so you can be a little slut and whore around."

I feel a sharp pain in my mouth as I bite down on my tongue. The bastard has always known exactly what to say to piss me off. I roll my shoulders and try to relax. I'm tired. All I wanna do is get out of these clothes, get a few hours of sleep, and then get back up to the hospital to spend some time with my father. "I'm not discussing this with you," I finally say as nicely as I can manage. "I'm going to bed. Show yourself out." First thing, when I get up later, is to call and have the locks changed. I haven't had the time to do it with all that has happened with my dad.

I turn around, but before I can take a step, his hand lands on my shoulder and I'm yanked back. *Wrong move!* I'm in no mood for him right now. Without thought, I rear my hand back and punch the motherfucker in the face.

CHAPTER THREE

"10-105," *Deceased body.* I hear an officer say into his radio as he stands to the right of me in the middle of the highway. I swallow thickly at what that means. I hear it so often, yet it still affects me. Still makes me sick to my stomach.

Wreckage.

Violence.

Blood.

Victims.

All of these things equal total chaos. It would amaze you how much cruelty there is in this world. You may lie in your comfy bed at night with your loved one next to you as you see it on your TV and think *oh my God, how does someone do that to another*? But I live it. I see it every single day. And it never gets any easier. No matter what they tell you or try to prepare you for in training, a person does not acclimate to the horrors that I see when I'm on a shift.

Being a police officer takes a certain type of person. And there are times that I feel like I may not be that person. I'm a grown-ass man and even I will admit that I have shed a tear or two. I'm not heartless by any means—although I know some women who may beg to differ with me on that. Don't get me wrong, I can be a total dick.

But as I stand here in the middle of a highway, sweating in my uniform even though it's the early morning, I look at the traffic backed up for miles. People just trying to make it to their everyday boring jobs. I wonder how many take their life for granted. I wonder how many are living in a loveless marriage, or how many times they've been in love. That thought makes me think of my parents. I immediately push that thought away. This is not the time and place for my personal issues.

I sigh heavily as my eyes drop to the carnage that lies at my feet—nothing but broken glass and shattered dreams of a little girl and my heart breaks.

She was two.

A two-year-old little girl who wore a pink Disney princess dress that was glittered in sparkles was killed only minutes ago. I'll never forget that for as long as I live. She looked so peaceful yet destroyed at the same time. It made me sick. She'll never have the chance to grow up. She'll never have the chance to fall in love. She'll never have the chance to be a mommy herself. All because her father didn't place her in her car seat correctly.

He survived—it's usually the ones who aren't responsible for the act that pay the price. He wasn't drunk or under the influence of any drugs. He is a normal guy working two jobs trying to support his family. He fell asleep on the way to drop his daughter off at daycare so he could get to his morning job on time and hit a guardrail. Although he was not wearing his seatbelt, the airbags were still able to save his life. Their little girl, however, was thrown from the car and died on impact.

Calls like this stay with you forever. No matter how much time passes the memory will always remain as if it was just yesterday—the ones you couldn't save.

I breathe heavily as I run from my cop car, arriving at the traffic scene. An SUV sits upside down in the middle of the lanes and the family's personal belongings scatter the highway. I see a little girl lying face down in a puddle of blood to my right and a man lying on his back as he screams out. Two guys try to hold him down while another officer tries to talk to him.

"Sir," the officer shouts trying to get his attention.

"Oh, my God," he cries. "Sarah," he screams as he looks over at the little girl lying in the middle of the road. "Please." He closes his eyes tightly. "Please God no." His body shakes.

I kneel down beside him as I look over his cut and bloodied face. He looks up at me, and he reaches up to grab my arm. His hand shakes and red tears run from his green eyes. "Please help her," he sobs. "I didn't mean to do it." He shakes his head. "It was an accident."

I nod my head as I try to give him words of encouragement, but nothing comes out. I know she's dead, and he knows she's dead. I can't save her. There's nothing I can do to help him.

The ambulance arrived then and took him to the hospital. We covered up the little girl until the coroner showed up.

Now I continue to stand here with a heavy heart.

"We need to wrap this up," Bobby, an officer, says looking at what's left of the family's SUV. Red pieces of the door lie only inches from my shoes. Glass litters the road and the wadded up SUV lies upside down across two lanes. "Cars are backed up more than two miles."

His concern for the traffic pisses me off. "So what?" I scowl. "The fuckers will be late to work." I shrug carelessly. At least they'll get there safe and sound. "The tow truck is on its way," I say as I turn to walk away.

I take a few steps and look down when I feel something under my boot. My throat tightens when I see a little pink blanket with a unicorn in the brightest yellow on it. I bend down and pick it up. I give it a shake to remove the glass and broken pieces of the car, but the blood of the child remains on it.

It breaks my heart to think of what her mother and father are going through right now. No parent should ever have to go through this — losing a child.

I fold the blanket up and carry it with me back to my patrol car.

I get into my car and dispatch comes through my radio, "10-16 in progress." Then they proceed to give me the location. *Domestic trouble.* Great! Just what I wanna fucking deal with right now.

I sigh heavily as I look at my watch. I've been off for over an hour. I'm tired and I'm grouchy as fuck. But that's part of the job.

"2388 In route," I say as I get the location before pulling away from the scene that will continue to haunt me.

I slow down as I come through the nice neighborhood—definitely upper class. It's probably some housewife who allows her wealthy-ass husband to beat on her. I'm not trying to stereotype, but I see it all the time.

I pull up to the house that already has one cop car. A man is standing outside—his white shirt shredded as it hangs off of his chest and shoulders. His jeans dirty and falling off his body. His face is red with rage while a police officer that I know well by the name of Jimmy is standing in front of him as he speaks. I get out of my car and the guy is screaming.

"That is mine. I'm here to get it. As soon as I get it—I'm out of here," he says pointing over the shoulder of the officer.

"What's the problem?" I ask walking over to them.

Jimmy the officer I know looks to me. "He and his girlfriend got into it. She wouldn't allow him to leave."

Girlfriend? If he looks like that, then she must look like shit. He doesn't seem like he would just sit back and take whatever a woman would dish out. I look the guy up and down with a scowl before I turn around in a circle looking over the very well-manicured, vacant front yard. "Looks like she's not here to stop you," I state, and Jimmy rolls his eyes. I have a problem with getting into trouble on the force. I'm not the best guy to send on a domestic dispute. I tend to make matters worse sometimes. My boss calls me a liability. I call it getting into character. Obviously, we have different opinions on how I need to handle things.

"She won't let me have my truck," he says pointing to the blue Chevy once again that sits in the driveway. He reminds me of a child—mad because his mother won't let him play with his favorite toy.

"That's because it's not yours."

I turn around when I hear a woman's voice. Normally a woman in hooker heels and Daisy dukes would turn me on. But at the moment, I'm tired as hell and the fact that I just saw a little girl die has me on edge. I'm in no mood to put up with a couple who wants to fight out in their front yard only to make up tomorrow.

"What is going on?" I ask her, placing my hands on my belt.

She looks over at me and her dark eyes look me up and down with a scowl—as if I am a fucking rent-a-cop. I square my shoulders and bow my chest out. I don't have time to mess with some bitch on a soapbox. And I sure as hell am in no mood.

She walks over to the Chevy, places her left arm on it, and leans up against it as if cool as a cucumber. It's irritating.

"That's my truck. I'm here to get it," the guys says angrily.

She shakes her head. "I bought you that truck."

"It's in my name," he argues.

"It's in both of our name you jackass," she replies with an eye roll. "And this house is in my name so it's sitting on my property. Get your ass off of it," she snaps.

I hold my hand up. "Wait..." I say turning to him. "You said she won't let you leave," I say as I scratch my head confused. Did I hear him right a while ago? I am going on a twelve-hour shift and living off espresso shots from the drive-thru of Starbucks. I tend to hear things wrong at times— another reason why my boss calls me a liability.

"What?" she screeches. "You told them I wouldn't let you leave?" she asks as she throws her hands around in the air. "I told you to get off of my fucking property. And what do you do? You call the fucking cops," she yells.

I turn to face him to tell him that he needs to vacate the property, but I stop when his eyes widen to the size of quarters. "NO!" he yells.

Jimmy and I spin back around in time to see her exiting the garage with a bat in her hand. She drives the thing into the driver's side of the door.

"You fucking bitch!" he yells as he starts to run

to her. Jimmy grabs him and pulls him down to the ground.

"Sir. I need you to calm down."

She places the ball of the bat on the ground and looks down at him with a smirk. "Still want it now?"

This chick is crazy! Like she eats a bowl of crazy for breakfast.

"Ma'am," I say lifting my hand showing her that I haven't pulled my gun out yet. I really don't want to have to do the paperwork that goes along with shooting someone tonight. "You don't need to vandalize the truck." There's no way we can make her give it up to him. This is something that will have to be addressed in a civil suit.

She snorts. "I know," she says as she continues to look down at her husband, boyfriend, whatever he is.

"Well..." I say trying to find the right words. This chick is a total bitch. And I'm running out of patience.

"Just give it to me. I'll leave," he says as he struggles underneath Jimmy.

She shakes her head and then walks back into the garage and I turn to face him as Jimmy allows him to get up.

"Do you live here, sir?" I ask him.

"The bitch kicked me out two days ago," he whines as he shakes Jimmy off him.

"Yet you keep coming back. Like a fucking

cockroach."

I turn back around and see her as she walks out of the garage once again. She pulls a knife out of her back pocket and before I can do anything, she stabs it into the front tire of the truck.

The guy runs past me and yanks her by the back of her top. He yanks her backward down onto the grass.

"You fucking bitch," he screams in her face.

She lands a punch to his nose before I can yank him off her. I toss him over to Jimmy as I reach down to help her up. Her eyes narrow at me, and she shoves my hand away. "Stay out of this," she growls as she shoots up to her feet.

Jimmy is in the process of putting the guy in handcuffs for assault when she runs toward him.

I tackle her to the ground before she can get to them. We hit hard as I knock her face down, her body under mine has her taking most of the blow.

"Get off me you son of a bitch," she yells as she claws at the grass trying to get away from me.

I reach up, grab her arms, and force them behind her back. It's not hard.

She's small, and well, I'm a man. I don't plan to arrest her; technically, she hasn't done anything wrong. She wants to fuck up her own shit—well then she's stupid but that's not illegal.

I lean down toward her trying to place my weight on her to keep her from squirming. "Just calm down..."

BAM! She lifts up and knocks the back of her head into my face making my eyes instantly water and my head hurt.

"Crazy fucking bitch," I hiss placing my knee into her back allowing me to get place handcuffs on her. Once done, I place my knee on her back to hold her down as I run my hand down my face and it comes up bloody.

"She is a crazy bitch." Her—whatever he is—says from across the lawn as he rests down on his knees with his hands cuffed behind his back. "She tried to chop my dick off this morning with a butter knife."

"Not like you need that five inches," she yells.

I watch as Jimmy's eyes widen at her words. I bend down, yanking her up by her cuffed arms. "You're under arrest...." I read her Miranda rights as I walk her back to Jimmy's car. I throw her into the backseat as she yells at her boyfriend to go fuck himself. I slam the door in her face.

Running a hand down my face once again, I cringe from how sore my nose is. "Am I still bleeding?" I ask as I tilt my head back for Jimmy to get a look at it.

He smirks. "Yeah."

"Fucking bitch," I curse, and the guy still kneeling on the grass nods his head in agreement.

"What are you doing here anyway?" Jimmy asks. "Are you on day shift now?"

I shake my head. "No. I just finished cleaning up the wreck on I-55." I tell him as I gently rub my nose with the back of my hand.

"Oh. I heard that one was bad."

I nod. "It was." It makes you sick how careless people can be. Take these two idiots, for example. They are fighting over a truck when the mother of that little girl is getting the news that her baby is dead and her husband was the reason for it. Sometimes I hate this job.

"Well, don't worry about me. They're both in handcuffs now, and there is another car on its way to help me take them in."

"Paperwork..."

"I'll take care of it. No worries." He nods to my car. "Go home and get some rest. You're gonna need it," he says looking down at my bloody nose.

"Go ahead and go home." He gestures to my cop car.

"Thank you," I say letting out a long breath. I'm so tired I could lay down and fall asleep on their grass right now.

I nod my head and thank him one more time before I head back to my car and head home. I'm tired and now I have a fucking headache from hell.

If you want to know more about Parker make sure to join his Facebook group- Parker's Pussies.

Want more of the Undescribable series? Tate and Missy's story, Unforgettable is available on Amazon and B&N as well as iBooks. Unpredictable, Parker's book is also available on Amazon and B&N. You can add them to you TBR list on Goodreads.

ABOUT THE AUTHOR

Shantel is a Texas born girl who now lives in Tulsa, Oklahoma with her high school sweetheart, who is a wonderful, supportive husband and their three year old little princess. She loves to spend time cuddled up on the couch with a good book.

She is currently working on her eighth book. She considers herself extremely lucky to get to be a stay at home wife and mother. Going to concerts and the movies are just a few of her favorite things to do. She hates coffee, but loves wine. She and her husband are both huge football fans, college and NFL. And she has to feed her high heel addiction by shopping for shoes weekly.

Although she has a passion to write, her family is most important to her. She loves spending evenings at home with her husband and daughter, along with their cat and dog.

For more information about the author and her books, visit her website-www.shanteltessierauthor.com. You can sign up for her newsletter on her website or follow her on Facebook and Twitter. The newsletter is the only place to get exclusive teasers, be the first to know about current projects and release dates, and also have chances to win some awesome giveaways.

Other Books by Shantel Tessier

Samantha and Slade's story
Undescribable
Unbearable
Uncontrollable
Unchangeable- Valentin's novella

Tate and Missy's story
Unforgettable
Unforeseen- Novella

Parker and Katherine's story
Unpredictable
DASH series.
DASH one
DASH two